Chicago Browning society

Robert Browning's Poetry

Outline studies

Chicago Browning society

Robert Browning's Poetry
Outline studies

ISBN/EAN: 9783337313241

Printed in Europe, USA, Canada, Australia, Japan

Cover: Foto ©Andreas Hilbeck / pixelio.de

More available books at **www.hansebooks.com**

Robert Browning's Poetry

" The development of a soul ; little else is worth study "

Outline Studies

PUBLISHED FOR THE CHICAGO BROWNING SOCIETY

CHICAGO
CHARLES H. KERR & COMPANY
175 Dearborn Street
1886

CONTENTS.

THESE outlines have been prepared with the hope that they may help in the study of a poet whose works evince the highest poetic art and insight, works which are so numerous and varied in character that they constitute, as Canon Farrar says, "a literature in themselves."

The order in which the poems of Robert Browning shall be studied is an important question, though fortunately one that permits of various answers, each of which will yield good results. The order set forth in the accompanying outline is the result of considerable experience as well as much thought, and it is hoped will commend itself to many. But others will prefer to begin with the love poems or the dramas, which display the poet's most characteristic quality. He is always dramatic Whatever form or style he uses, his writings are everywhere permeated by the spirit of a living, struggling humanity.

> *"Man's thoughts and loves and hates.
> Earth is my vineyard, these grew there."

One club in New York began with "Sordello" and courageously carried the study through three years, although it is the poem upon which chiefly rests the poet's reputation for obscurity. Other classes have begun with "The Ring and The Book."

Whatever order is pursued, the student of Browning, like that of any other poet, had better pursue his work in his own way. The best results are attained in the open mind, equally devoid of prejudice and conceit, which acquires its own power of judging and makes its own application of the truths and lessons taught.

*Epilogue to Pacchiarotto.

A CLASSIFICATION

Of the entire writings of Robert Browning, arranged for the guidance of clubs and classes, with a few notes added, containing information not found in the text.

Those shrinking from the long course can readily and profitably elect such numbers as attract them.

The abbreviations refer to titles of books in the American edition. See chronological list, page 35.

i.

1. **Biography and Bibliography of Browning.** (*a.*)
2. **Popular Poems.**
   ✓ The Pied Piper of Hamelin. D. P. (*b.*)
   The Boy and the Angel. D. P. (*c.*)
   The Twins. M. and W. (*d.*)
   . ✓ How They brought the Good News from Ghent
      to Aix. D. P. (*e.*)

(*a.*) See article by E. W. Gosse in *Scribner's*, Dec. 1881; London Browning Society Papers, Part I; " Poets and Problems," by George W. Cooke; Stedman's " Victorian Poets." A good portrait of the poet is published in Illustrations, Part II. L. B. S.

(*b.*) Written for the little son of the actor, William Macready.

(*c.*) Compare Longfellow's " King Robert of Sicily."

(*d.*) This parable is told by Martin Luther in his " Table Talk." This poem was published with Mrs. Browning's " A Plea for the Ragged Schools of London." " These two poems were printed by Miss Arabella Barrett, Mrs. Browning's sister, for a bazaar to benefit the ' Refuge for Young Destitute Girls,' one of the first refuges of the kind, and still in existence."—*London Browning Society Papers.*

(5)

(*e.*) This ride is supposed to have occurred during the Dutch war of Independence, early in the seventeenth century. The following extract is from a letter written by Mr. Browning: "There is no sort of historical foundation about ' Good News from Ghent.' I wrote it under the bulwark of a vessel off the African coast, after I had been at sea long enough to appreciate even the fancy of a gallop on the back of a certain good horse ' York,' then in my stable at home."

II.

Poems of Heroism.

1. Incident of a French camp. D. P. (*a.*)
2. Pheidippides. Ag. (*b.*)
3. Echetlos. Ag. (*c.*)
4. Hervé Riel. F. (*d.*)
5. Tray. Ag. (*e.*)
6. The Patriot. M. & W. (*f.*)
7. Clive. Ag. (*g.*)
8. The Lost Leader. (*h.*)·

(*a.*) The story of this poem is true with the exception that its hero was not a boy but a full-grown man.

(*b.*) " The facts related in ' Pheidippides ' belong to Greek legendary history and are told by Herodotus and other writers. When Athens was threatened by the invading Persians, she sent a running messenger to Sparta to demand help against the foreign foe. The mission was unsuccessful but the runner Pheidippides fell in on his return with the god Pan; and although alone among Greeks, the Athenians had refused to honor him, he promised to fight with them in the coming battle. Pheidippides was present when this battle—that of Marathon—was fought and won."—*Mrs. Orr's " Handbook."*

He ran once again and announced the victory at Athens. The release from toil which Pan promised him as a reward for his labors was not the release he had expected. Marathon was well-known as the "fennel-field."

(*c.*) This is another legend of the battle of Marathon. The word "Echetlos" means "Holder of the Ploughshare." A picture of Echetlos was in Athens.

(*d.*) A true story of 1692.

(*e.*) This scene really occurred in Paris. The poem is a biting sarcasm, directed against vivisection, which the poet has repeatedly called "an infamous practice."

(*f.*) In the first edition the scene of this poem was laid in Brescia, but subsequently the name of the city was omitted and the significance of its universal application thereby heightened.

(*g.*) "That part of the poem, in which Clive says that if the bully had, instead of confessing himself a cheat, pardoned Clive and spared his life, he should have picked up the weapon cast away by his foe and used it on himself, is Browning's own invention. He considered it a legitimate deduction from the fact that, when Clive had to face an inquiry into his conduct, he destroyed himself. On the day of Lord Clive's death, a lady, who was staying in the house, asked him to come in and mend a pen for her. Such was his nerve that he did so and then went into the next room and cut his throat with the very penknife he had used in her service."—*L. Br. S. Papers.*

(*h.*) Refers to Wordsworth, for his defection, with Southey and others, from the liberal cause.

III.

Art—Poetry and Poets.

1. How It Strikes A Contemporary. M. and W.
2. Transcendentalism. M. and W. (*a.*)
3. "Touch Him Ne'er So Lightly." Epilogue to Dramatic Idyls. Ag. (*b.*)
4. Memorabilia. M. and W.
5. Epilogue to Pacchiarotto. (*c.*)
7. At The Mermaid. Pac. (*d.*)
8. House. Pac. (*e.*)
9. Popularity. M. and W. (*f.*)

(*a.*) Johannes Teutonicus, a canon of Halberstadt, in Germany, after he had performed a number of prestigious feats almost incredible, was transported by the Devil in the likeness of a black horse, and was both seen and heard upon one and the same Christmas Day to say mass in Halberstadt, in Mayntz and in Cologne."—*Heywood's* "*Hierarchy,*" *Book IV.*

(*b.*) These lines were taken by critics as referring to Browning's own poetry. On writing them again in the album of Mrs. R. H. Dana (Miss Edith Longfellow) he added the following lines:

Thus I wrote in London, musing on my betters,
Poets dead and gone; and lo, the critics cried,
"Out on such a boast!" as if I dreamed that fetters
Binding Dante, bind up me! as if true pride
Were not also humble!

So I smiled and sighed
As I oped your book in Venice this bright morning,
Sweet, new friend of mine! and felt the clay or sand—
Whatsoe'er my soil be,—break—for praise or scorning—
Out in grateful fancies—weeds, but weeds expand
Almost into flowers, held by such a kindly hand.

(*c.*) This is spoken directly by Mr. Browning himself and is a criticism of his critics. The words "The poets pour us wine" at the beginning of the poem are quoted from Mrs. Browning's "Wine of Cyprus."

(*d.*) Browning speaks here behind the mask of Shakespeare. To "throw Venus" was to throw the highest cast at Roman dice.

(*e.*) See Wordsworth's Sonnet, "Scorn not the Sonnet."

(*f.*) Compare George Eliot's "Jubal."

IV.

Art—Poetry Continued.

1. The Two Poets of Croisic. Ag. (*a.*)
2. Essay on Shelley. B. S. Papers. (*b.*)

(*a.*) Le Croisic is situated in the southeastern corner of Brittany. Sardine fishing and the crystallization of sea salt are still the chief occupations of the villagers. René Gentilhomme lived in the first half of the seventeenth century, and Paul Desforges Maillard about a hundred years later. The story of the later poet forms the subject of a famous play, Piron's "Métromanie."

(*b.*) The Essay on Shelley was written about the year 1851 to serve as an introduction to some Shelley Letters. These letters were afterwards discovered to be a forgery and the book was suppressed, but they gave Browning a chance of writing about the art of the poet he admired.

V.

Art—Painting and Painters.
1. Fra Lippo Lippi. M. and W. (*a.*)
2. Andrea del Sarto. M. and W. (*b.*)
3. The Guardian Angel. M. and W. (*c.*)
4. Pictor Ignotus. D. P.

(*a.*) The story of the life of this well-known painter, as told here by himself, is historical, even to the incident of the escapade from the palace of Cosmo de Medici, who had shut him up to finish his painting. The picture which he describes is that of "The Coronation of the Virgin," still in Florence. "Hulking Tom" was the painter known as Masaccio. See Lowell's poem of that name.

(*b.*) The facts related here are also historical in substance, though certain chroniclers present the character of Lucrezia more favorably. The king was Francis I.

(*c.*) This describes an actual picture, imputed to Guercino and now in the church of St. Augustine at Fano on the coast of Italy. The "Alfred" of the same poem is the friend referred to in the poem of "Waring"—Alfred Domett, then prime minister of New Zealand. The London Browning Society have published photograph illustrations of this picture, also of Andrea del Sarto's picture of himself and his wife in the Pitti gallery at Florence, which suggested the poem, and Fra Lippo's picture of the "Coronation."

VI.

Art—Painting and Sculpture.
1. Old Pictures in Florence. M. and W. (*a.*)
2. Eurydice. (*b.*)
3. A Face. D. P.
4. Deaf and Dumb. A Group by Woolner. (*c.*)

(*a.*) Stanzas 26, 27, 28. Bijordi is the family name of "Domenico," called "Ghirlandajo" from the family trade of wreath-making. "Landro" stands for Alessandro Botticelli. "Lippino" was son of Fra Lippo Lippi. Mr. Browning alludes to him as "wronged," because others were credited with some of his best work.   Lorenzo Monaco (the monk) was a contemporary, or nearly so, of Fra Angelico, but more severe in manner.   "Pollajolo" was both painter and sculptor.   "Margheritone of Arezzo" was one of the earlier Old Masters and died, as Vasari states, *infastidito* (deeply annoyed) by the success of Giotto and the "new school," hence the funeral garb in which Mr. Browning depicts him.

"Mr. Browning possesses or possessed pictures by all the artists mentioned in this connection."—*Mrs. Orr.*

The translations of Vasari (which may be found in Bohn's Standard Library) give accounts of three painters.

The story of Giotto's O is told in every description of the painter, but the fact that in some editions O was misprinted "Oh" might cause some confusion.

The "dotard," who was to be pitched across the Alps before freedom could be restored to Florence and art revive, was the Grand Duke.

(*b.*) This poem is not included in the American edition of Browning's works.   It is the poet's interpretation of a picture by F. Leighton.

> "But give them me—the mouth, the eyes, the brow!
> Let them once more absorb me!   One look now
>   Will lap me round forever, not to pass
> Out of its light, though darkness lie beyond!
> Hold me but safe again within the bond
>   Of one immortal look! all woe that was
> Forgotten, and all terror that may be
> Defied; no past is mine, no future!   Look at me!"

(*c.*) This poem is also unfortunately omitted from certain editions. It consists of eight lines written for Woolner's group of Constance and Arthur, the deaf and dumb children of Sir Thomas Fairbairn. The group was exhibited in the International Exhibition of 1862.

> "Only the prism's obstruction shows aright
> The secret of a sunbeam, breaks its light
> Into the jeweled bow from blankest white :
>   So may a glory from defect arise:
> Only by Deafness may the vexed Love wreak
> Its insuppressive sense on brow and cheek,
> Only by Dumbness adequately speak
>   As favored mouth could never, through the eyes."

VII.

Art.—Music.

1. A Toccata of Galluppi's.   M. and W. (*a.*)
2. Master Hugues of Saxe Gotha.   M. and W.
3. Abt Vogler.   D. P.

(*a.*) "The Venetian Baldassarre Galuppi, surnamed Buranello, was an immensely prolific composer, and abounded in melody, tender, pathetic and brilliant."—*Studies of the Eighteenth Century in Italy, by Vernon Lee.*

(*b.*) The Abbé Vogler lived from 1749 to 1814, and was the master of great musicians, including Von Weber and Meyerbeer.   It is fitting that he should have been taken as the type of a great extemporizer, since none of his work survives.   The beauty and meaning of the poem do not depend in the least on historical associations connected with the name.

VIII.

Love.

1. By the Fireside.   M. and W. (*a.*)
2. In Three Days.   M. and W.
3. One Word More.   M. and W. (*b.*)
4. O Lyric Love.   R. and B.   Book I., lines 1391 to 1416; Book XII., lines 865 to 870. (*c.*)
5. Apparitions.   The Prologue to Two Poets of Croisic.   Ag.
6. Never the Time or the Place.   J.
7. Wanting—is What?   J.
8. A Wall.   Prologue to Pacchiarotto.

(*a.*) These are the poems generally accepted as written directly to Mrs. Browning.   Notice in "By the Fireside" the poet's plan for work to be done some time in Greek literature, which he has since carried out.

(*b.*) This form of blank verse which the poet uses here, "the first time and the last time," is so musical that one never misses the rhyme. Bice is a common abbreviation for Beatrice.

(*c.*) With this invocation in mind, it is interesting to study all the prologues and epilogues of the books Browning has published since.

IX.

Love—Mutual Love.

1. Meeting at Night. D. P.
2. Parting at Morning. D. P.
3. Love Among the Ruins. M. and W.
4. Mesmerism. M. and W.
5. A Lover's Quarrel. M. and W.
6. The Flower's Name. D. P.
7. Respectability. M. and W.
8. In a Gondola. D. P. (*a.*)

(*a.*) This poem was suggested by a picture of Maclise.

X.

I. Love—Self Renunciation.

1. The Lost Mistress. D. P.
2. The Last Ride Together. M. and W.
3. A Serenade at the Villa. M. and W.

II. Love—Unsatisfied.

1. Two in the Campagna. M. and W.
2. A Pretty Woman. M. and W.
3. Youth and Art. D. P.
4. St. Martin's Summer. Pac.

XI.

Love—The Woman's Side.

1. In a Year. M. and W.
2. A Woman's Last Word. M. and W.
3. Any Wife to Any Husband. M. and W.
4. James Lee's Wife. D. P. (*a.*)

(*a.*) The wife speaks throughout. This poem is interesting in representing different periods in the poet's life and power. The song in Part VI. was written by Browning in 1836—the poem itself published in 1864; important additions made in Part VIII. in 1872, not in American edition, found in Crowell's "Red Line" selections, and in L. Br. S. Papers, Part I., p. 59.

XII.

Love—On One Side.

1. Rudel to the Lady of Tripoli. D. P. (*a.*)
2. Cristina. D. P. (*b.*)
3. Mary Wollstonecraft and Fuseli. J.
4. A Likeness. D. P.
5. Numpholeptos. Pac.

(*a.*) Rudel was a troubadour of the twelfth century, and it is related in "Tales of the Troubadours" that he loved the Lady of Tripoli.

(*b.*) This was meant for a young man who fell in love with Queen Cristina of Spain and became insane.—*L. Br. S. Papers.*

XIII.

Love—Incomplete.

1. The Statue and the Bust. M. and W. (*a.*)
2. The Worst of it. D. P.
3. Too Late. D. P.

4. Dis Alitur Visum. Le Byron de Nos Jours. D. P.
5. Bifurcation.   Pac.
6. Appearances.   Pac.
7. Confessions.   D. P.

(*a.*) The Bust was invented by Browning. The Statue is that of the " Great-Duke Ferdinand " in the square of the Santissima Annunziata in Florence.   According to tradition, the duke loved a lady who lived in the Riccardi Palace, at one corner of the square, whom he could see only at her window, and that he had his statue placed where it would look in that direction.   Browning tells us that the bust was executed in della Robia ware.   Specimens of this work adorn the cornice of the palace.

"The crime alluded to in the poem as darkening the Medici palace, and casting its shadow on the adjacent street, was the murder of Alexander, Duke of Florence, in 1836."—*Mrs Orr.*

This is written in the Italian *terza rima*, and is a good illustration of Browning's facility in difficult meters.

XIV.

Love—Tragedy.

✓1. Porphyria's Lover.   D. P.
2. Martin Relph.   Ag.
3. A Forgiveness.   Pac. (*a.*)
✓4. The Laboratory.   D. P.
✓5. The Confessional.
6. Cristina and Monaldeschi. (*b.*)

(*a.*) Mr Browning owns a collection of "arms of eastern workmanship," just such as is described here.

(*b.*) An interesting description of Queen Cristina may be found in "Madame de Sevigné and her Contemporaries," by Mlle. de Montpensier.   Avon is the village on the east side of the park of Fontainebleau.   Monaldeschi was buried in its little church.

XV.

Love.

1. In a Balcony. M. and W.

Give special attention to the different character-studies. Constance and the Queen are among the most subtile characters in Browning.

XVI.

Love Lyrics.

1. Misconceptions. M. and W.
2. My Star. M. and W.
3. Love in a Life. M. and W.
4. Life in a Love. M. and W.
5. One Way of Love. M. and W.
6. Another Way of Love. M. and W.
7. Women and Roses. M. and W.
8. Natural Magic. Pac.
9. Magical Nature. Pac.
10. Song. D. P.
11. Earth's Immortalities, II. Love. D. P.

XVII.

Jewish Poems.

1. Holy Cross Day. M. and W.
2. Filippo Baldinucci on the Privilege of Burial. Pac. (*a.*)
3. Jochanan Hakkadosh. J. (*b.*)

(*a.*) " Filippo Baldinucci was the author of a history of art, and the incident which Mr. Browning relates as a reminiscence of A. D. 1670, appears there in a notice of the life of the painter Buti."—*Mrs. Orr.*

(*b.*) In the note at the conclusion of the poem "Mr. Browning professes to rest his narrative on a Rabbinical work, of which the title, given by him in Hebrew, means 'Collection of many lies;' and he adds, by way of supplement, three sonnets, supposed to illustrate the equally fictitious proverb ' From Moses to Moses, never was one like Moses,' and embodying as many fables of wildly increasing audacity. The main story is nevertheless justified by traditional Jewish belief."

" The three days' survival of the ' Ruach' or spirit allowed to departed saints, is a Talmudic doctrine still held among the Jews.

" The ' Helaphta ' was a noted Rabbi.   The ' Bier ' and the ' Three Daughters' was a received Jewish name for the constellation of the Great Bear.   The ' Salem ' is the mystical New Jerusalem to be built of the spirits of the great and good."—*Mrs. Orr.*

XVIII.

Early Christian Poems.

1. Cleon.   M. and W. (*a.*)
2. An Epistle.   M. and W.
3. A Death in the Desert.   D. P. (*b.*)

(*a.*) The line from the address of Paul to the Athenians—Acts xvii., 28—indicates that Cleon is supposed to be one of those Greek poets, living at the very time Paul is preaching the doctrine of the resurrection of the dead.

(*b.*) " This is the record of an imaginary last scene in the life of St. John   It is conceived in perfect harmony with the facts of the case; the great age which the Evangelist attained; the mystery which shrouded his death; the persecutions which had overtaken the church; the heresies which already threatened to disturb it; but Mr. Browning has given to his St. John a fore-knowledge of that age of philosophic doubt in which its very foundations would be shaken."— *Mrs. Orr.*

This poem was the poet's contribution to the discussion that was aroused by the appearance of Strauss's " Life of Jesus."

XIX.

Other Religious Poems.

1. The Heretic's Tragedy; a Middle-Age Interlude. M. and W. (*a.*)

2. Johannes Agricola in Meditation.   D. P. (*b.*)
3. Christmas Eve.   D. P.
4. Easter Day.   D. P.
5. Fears and Scruples.   Pac.
6. Epilogue to Dramatis Personæ.

(*a.*) "This heretic is Jacques du Bourg-Molay, last Grand Master of the Order of Knights Templar, against whom preposterous accusations had been brought.   This Jacques, whom the speaker erroneously calls 'John,' and who might stand for any victim of middle-age fanaticism, was burned in Paris in 1314; and the 'Interlude,' we are told, 'would seem to be a reminiscence of this event, as distorted by two centuries of refraction from Flemish brain to brain.'"—*Mrs. Orr.*

(*b.*) "The speaker, Johannes Agricola, was a German reformer of the sixteenth century, and alleged founder of the sect of the Antinomians; a class of Christians who extended the Low Church doctrine of the insufficiency of good works, and declared the children of God to be exempt from the necessity of performing them."—*Mrs. Orr.*

XX.

Other Religious Poems.

1. Caliban.
2. Saul. (*a.*)

(*a.*) Compare the fifth stanza with Matthew Arnold's "Empedocles on Ætna," especially for the description of the effect of music on disordered mental conditions.

XXI.

Death and Immortality.

1. Prospice.   D. P. (*a.*)
2. Apparent Failure.   D. P. (*b.*)
3. Pisgah Sights.   Pac. (*c.*)
4. La Saisiaz.   Ag. (*d.*)

✓5. Evelyn Hope.   M. and W.

✓6. Rabbi Ben Ezra.   D. P. *(e.)*

7. Jochanan Hakkadosh.

(a.) This is one of the " E. B. B." poems.   Compare with Pope's " Dying Christian," and Bryant's " Thanatopsis."

(b.) " Mr. Browning's verdict on three drowned men, whose bodies he saw exposed at the morgue in Paris, in the summer of 1856." —*Mrs. Orr.*

(c.) These can hardly be called poems of death, or immortality. They belong at least to that class, where death is the interpreter of life.

(d.) "A. E. S. were the initials of Miss Anne Egerton Smith, the proprietress of the *Liverpool Mercury,* who was at La Saisiaz with Browning and his sister, and whose sudden death gave rise to the poem."—*L., Br. S. Papers.*

" La Saisiaz" is Savoyard for " The Sun," and is the name of a villa among the mountains near Geneva.

(e.) Rabbi Ben Ezra was one of the four great philosophers or Lights of the Jews in the middle ages, and lived from 1092 to 1167. He was born in Toledo, Spain, but traveled through many lands, including England.   He believed in a future life.   This poem, though put into the mouth of the Jewish teacher, is too great to be classed among the Jewish poems.   It has been said to contain " the whole philosophy of life."   Compare the potter's song with Longfellow's "Keramos," and the " Rubaiyat" of Omar Khayam.

XXII.

Romantic.

✓ 1. Childe Roland.   M. and W. *(a.)*

2. The Flight of the Duchess.   D. P.

3. The Glove.   D. P.

4. Count Gismond.   D. P.

5. The Italian in England.   D. P. *(b.)*

6. Protus.   M. and W.

7. Gold Hair.   D. P. *(c.)*

(*a.*) "All Browning's great and peculiar qualities as a poet, find their fullest and most perfect expression in Childe Roland, which, as a feat of the imagination, surpasses in creative power, in range of thought and feeling, in vividness and dramatic interest any poem of its kind, which has been written since 'Cristabel' and 'The Ancient Mariner.' It is like these in its seeming supernatural aspect—I say seeming, because there is nothing in Childe Roland above and beyond nature if we start with the poet at the starting point, which is found near the end of the poem. The origin of the line from Shakespeare is found in no known ballad or poem, but it is probably from a lost part of 'Childe Rowland and Burd Helen.' The coming to the dark tower is not the beginning but the end of the story. The hero who reaches that goal and boldly asserts himself has won the crown—his very presence there is victory. These thirty-four stanzas have the substance of a poem or drama of large proportions."—*Richard Grant White.*

(*a.*) This poem was written in one day.
(*b.*) A fragment of an imaginary chronicle.
(*c.*) This story may be read in Pornic guide books.

XXIII.

Narrative.

1. Halbert and Hob. Ag.
2. Ned Bratts. Ag. (*a.*)
3. Pietro of Abano. (*b.*)
4. Ivan Ivanovitch.
5. Muleykeh.
6. Donald. J.

(*a.*) The main facts of this narrative are true, and related in a book by John Bunyan, as having happened in Hertford. "Mr. Browning has turned Hertford into Bedford; made the time of the occurrence coincide with that of Bunyan's imprisonment there; and supposed the evident conversion of this man and woman to be among the many which he effected."—*Mrs. Orr.*

(*b.*) "Pietro, of Abano, was an Italian physician and alchemist, born at Abano, near Paduain, 1246, died about 1320. He is said to have studied Greek at Constantinople, mathematics at Padua, and to have been made a doctor of medicine and philosophy at Paris. He then returned to Padua, where he was professor of medicine and followed the Arabian physicians, especially Averrhoes. He got a great reputation and charged enormous fees. He hated milk and cheese, and swooned at the sight of them. His enemies, jealous of his renown and wealth, denounced him to the Inquisition as a magician. They accused him of possessing the Philosopher's Stone, and of making, with the devil's help, all money come back to his purse. His trial was begun, and, had he not died naturally in time, he would have been burnt. The Inquisitors ordered his body to be burned, and as a friend had taken that away, they had his portrait publicly burned by the executioner. In 1560 a Latin epitaph in his memory was put up in the church of St. Augustin. The Duke of Urbino set his statue among those of illustrious men, and the Senate of Padua put one on the gate of its palace."—*L. Br. S. Papers.*

XXIV.

Friendship.

1. Waring. D. P.
2. May and Death. D. P. (*a.*)
3. Time's Revenges. D. P.
4. A Light Woman. M. and W.

(*a.*) "Surely the Polygonum Persicaria, or Spotted Persicaria, is the plant alluded to. It is a common weed with purple stains upon its rather large leaves; these spots varying in size and vividness of color, according to the nature of the soil where it grows. A legend attaches to this plant and attributes these stains to the blood of Christ having fallen on its leaves, growing below the cross."—*L. Br. S. Papers.*

This poem was a personal utterance, called forth by the death of a relative whom Mr. Browning dearly loved.

XXV.

Hate and Revenge.

1. Instans Tyrannus. M. and W. (*a*).
2. Before. M. and W.
3. After. M. and W.
4. Soliloquy of a Spanish Cloister.

(*a*.) "The 'present tyrant,' suggested by some words in Horace, 8th Ode, Book II. This is the confession of a king who has been possessed by an unreasoning and uncontrolled hatred of one man."—*Mrs. Orr.*

XXVI.

Poems of Humour.

1. Up at a Villa—Down in the City. M. and W.
2. Sibrandus Schafnaburgensis. D. P
3. Doctor ——. Ag. (*a*.)
4. Pacchiarotto. (*b*.)
5. Solomon and Balkis. J. (*c*.)
6. Adam, Lilith and Eve. J.
7. Pambo. J. (*d*.)

(*a*.) An old Hebrew legend, founded upon the saying that a bad wife is stronger than death. Satan complains in his character of death, that man has the advantage of him, since he may baffle him, whenever he will, by the aid of a bad woman. He undertakes to show this in his own person.

(*b*.) A painter of Siena, generally confounded with Girolamo del Pacchia. These incidents in the poem are historical, and related in Vasari.

(*c*.) The Talmudic version of the dialogue between Solomon and the queen of Sheba. The ring bore the Supreme name and compelled the person towards whom it was turned, to speak the truth.

(*d.*) The name of Pambo or Pambus is known to literature as that of a foolish person, who spent months, Mr. Browning says years, in the pondering a simple passage from Psalm 39.

XXVII.

National and Political Feeling.

1. Cavalier Tunes. D. P.
2. De Gustibus. M. and W.
3. Home Thoughts from Abroad. D. P.
4. Home Thoughts from the Sea. D. P. (*a.*)
5. The Italian in England. D. P.
6. The Englishman in Italy. D. P.
7. Through the Metidja to Abd-el-Kadr. D. P. (*b.*)

(*a.*) "Here and here" is said to refer to the battles of Cape St. Vincent (1796) and Trafalgar (1805), and perhaps to the defence of Gibraltar (1782).

(*b.*) This represents a follower of Abd-el-Kadr hastening through the desert to join his chief.

XXVIII.

Poems of the Renaissance.

1. The Bishop Orders His Tomb. D. P. (*a.*)
2. My Last Duchess. D. P.
3. The Grammarian's Funeral. M. and W.

(*a.*) The Bishop's tomb is entirely fictitious, but something which is made to stand for it is shown to credulous sight-seers in St. Praxed's Church at Rome.

See " Browning and the Critics," page 43.

XXIX.

Unclassified Poems.

1. Shop. Pac.
2. Epilogue to Two Poets of Croisic. Ag.
3. Earth's Immortalities; Fame. D. P.
4. Cenciaja. F. (*a.*)
5. Prologue and Epilogue to Fifine.

(*a.*) " Cenciaja" signifies matter relating to the Cenci; the word is also a pun on the meaning of the plural noun Cenci, rags or old rags. The cry of this, frequent in Rome, was at first mistaken by Shelley for a voice urging him to go on with his play. Mr. Browning has used it to indicate the comparative unimportance of his contribution to the Cenci story. The quoted Italian proverb means something to the same effect, that every trifle will press in for notice among worthier matters The poem describes an incident extraneous to the Cenci tragedy, but which strongly influenced its course.

XXX.

Special Pleadings.

1. Bishop Blougram's Apology. M. and W. (*a.*)
2. Mr. Sludge the Medium. D. P. (*b.*)
3. Prince Hohenstiel Schwangau. F. (*c.*)

(*a.*) The original of this poem was Cardinal Wiseman. It is said that the cardinal reviewed very good naturedly this poem in the " Rambler," a Romanist journal.

(*b.*) Home, the spiritualist, was the original of Sludge.

(*c.*) A defence of the doctrine of expediency, and the monologue is supposed to be carried on by the late emperor of the French. Hohen-Schwangau is one of the castles of the King of Bavaria. The " grim guardian of the square" refers to the statue of George First on horseback.

XXXI.

From Classic Sources.

1. Pan and Luna.   Ag. (*a.*)
2. Artemis Prologuizes.   D. P. (*b.*)
3. Ixion.   J.

(*a*) This mythical adventure of Luna, the moon, is described by Virgil in the Georgics.   The text is taken from the Georgics, " If it is worthy of belief."

(*b.*) "This was suggested by the Hippolytos of Euripides and destined to become part of a larger poem, which should continue its story, Hippolytos perishing through the anger of Venus, was revived by Artemis (Diana), and afterwards fell in love with one of her nymphs. Aricia.   Mr. Browning imagines that she has removed him in secret to her own forest retreat and is nursing him back to life by the help of Esculapius, and the poem is a monologue in which sh· describes what has passed since Phædra's self-betrayal to the present time. Hippolytos still lies unconscious, but the power of the great healer has been brought to bear on him, and the unconsciousness seems only that of sleep.   The ensuing chorus of nymphs, the awakening of Hippolytos, and with it the stir of the new passion with him, had already taken shape in Mr. Browning's mind.   Unfortunately something put the inspiration to flight, and it did not return."—*Mrs. Orr.*

XXXII.

Balaustion's Adventure.

This is a transcription of one of the plays of Euripides, placed in an original setting.   Balaustion herself is one of the freshest and most lyrical of Browning's creations.

"Balaustion is a Rhodian girl, brought up in the worship of Euripides.   The Peloponnesian war has entered upon its second stage, the Athenian fleet has been defeated at Syracuse, and Rhodes, resenting this disgrace, has determined to take part against Athens, and joins the Peloponnesian league.   But Balaustion will not forsake the mother city and persuades her kinsmen to migrate with her to it.

They take ship at Kaunus, but the wind turns them from their course and when it abates they find themselves in strange waters, pursued by a pirate bark. They fly before it towards what they hope will prove a friendly shore, Balaustion heartening the rowers by a song from Æschylus, sung at the battle of Salamis, and run into the hostile harbor of Syracuse, where shelter is denied them."—*Mrs. Orr.*

Balaustion means "wild pomegranate flower," and the girl has been so called on account of her lyric gifts.

The lines beginning "I know too a great Kaunian painter," refer to a picture by F. Leighton, called "Hercules wrestling with Death for the body of Alkestis," an engraving of which has been published by the London Browning Society.

XXXIII.

Aristophanes' Apology.

"In point of circumstance, a sequel to Balaustion's Adventure. Both turn on the historical fact that Euripides was reverenced far more by the non-Athenian Greeks than by the Athenians. Both contain a transcript from him."—*Mrs. Orr.*

XXXIV.

Agamemnon.

As a literal translation of one of the most difficult of the ancient Greek tragedies, Browning's Agamemnon deserves careful study in connection with other translations of the same work, but may be very properly omitted from a regular Browning course.

XXXV.

Dramas—Strafford.

This was written at a request of Macready and brought out by him at the Covent Garden Theatre in 1837. "Write me a play, Browning, and keep me from going to America." Browning calls this a play representing action in character, rather than character in action. The portraits in the play are historical with the exception of Lady Carlisle, which is purely imaginary. The Italian boat song in the last scene is from Redi's Bacco, translated by Leigh Hunt. "Strafford" has been edited with notes by Miss Hickey, with special reference to school and club study, and published in a small volume by itself.

XXXVI.

Dramas—Pippa Passes.

This drama illustrates the unconscious influence which a little silk-weaver, strolling happily along the country lanes during her brief holiday, exerts upon the character and actions of those who only hear her songs. The song, beginning " Give her but a least excuse to love me," refers to Catherine Cornaro, the Venetian queen of Cyprus, and is the only one of the songs which is based on any fact.

XXXVII.

Dramas—Luria.

This is supposed to be an episode in the struggles between Florence and Pisa.

" Luria is grave and somewhat remote; it simply represents Duty triumphing in the midst of intrigue, and with no motive beyond duty's self. The conception is grand, the result impressive—but it is a lesson; the ' Blot in the Scutcheon ' is an experience."—*John Weiss.*

It is interesting to note in connection with the passage where the secretary refers to the charcoal sketch of a Moorish front for the unfinished Duomo, that recently such a sketch has been actually found in the small museum, Opera del Duomo, at Florence. Browning did not know of its existence.

XXXVIII.

Dramas—Blot in the Scutcheon.

First produced at the Theatre Royal in 1853. Dickens said of this play, that he would rather have written it than any work of modern times.

XXXIX.

Dramas—Colombe's Birthday.

"Colombe of Ravestein is ostensibly duchess of Juliers and Cleves, but her title is neutralized by the Salic law under which the duchy is held; and though the duke, her late father, has wished to evade it in her behalf, those about her are aware that he had no power to do so, and that the legal claimant, her cousin, may at any moment assert his rights. This happens on the first anniversary of her accession, which is also her birthday."—*Mrs. Orr.*

XL.

Dramas—Paracelsus.

A dramatic poem in which the principal character is the celebrated empiric and alchemist of the sixteenth century. It has been pronounced by Weiss and others to be the loftiest effort of Browning's genius. Weiss says "We must not take Paracelsus as a drama, but a meditative poem too grave to entertain a reminiscence of the theatre."

XLI.

Dramas—King Victor and King Charles.

The story of this drama is historical, and can be found in a number of the histories of this period. Browning's justification of his own view of the characters is found in the preface to the play.

XLII.

Dramas—A Soul's Tragedy.

XLIII.

Dramas—The Return of the Druses.

"The Druses of Lebanon are a compound of several Eastern tribes, owing their religious system to a Caliph of Egypt, Hakeen Biamr

Allah, and probably their name to his confessor, Darazi, who first attempted to promulgate his doctrine among them; some also impute to the Druse nation a dash of the blood of the Crusaders. One of their chief religious doctrines was that of divine incarnations. It seems to have originated in the pretension of Hakeem to be himself one; and as organized by the Persian mystic, Hamzi, his vizier and disciple, it included ten manifestations of this kind, of which Hakeem must have formed the last. Mr. Browning has assumed that in any great national emergency the miracle would be expected to recur, and he has here conceived an emergency sufficiently great to call it forth."—*Mrs. Orr.*

XLIV.

Pauline.

"This poem is, as its title declares, a fragment of a confession. The speaker is a man, probably still young; and Pauline, the name of the lady who receives the confession and is supposed to edit it. It is not, however, 'fragmentary' in the sense of revealing only a small part of the speaker's life, or of only recording isolated acts from which the life may be built up. Its fragmentary character lies in this: that while very explicit as a record of feeling and motive, it is entirely vague in respect to acts. It is an elaborate retrospect of successive mental states big with the sense of corresponding misdeeds. An ultra-consciousness of self is in fact the key-note of the entire mental situation. [The life of Pauline's lover has not been wholly misspent, but his ultimate object has been always the gratification of self.] We leave him at the close of his confession, exhausted by the mental fever, but released from it—new-born to a better life; though how and why this has happened is again part of the mystery of the case. 'Pauline' is *the* one of Browning's longer poems, of which no intelligible abstract is possible: a circumstance the more striking, in that it is perfectly transparent as well as truly poetical so far as its language is concerned. * * *

" The defects and difficulties of Pauline are plainly admitted in an editor's note written in French and signed by this name: and which, proceeding as it does from the author himself, supplies a valuable comment on the work. * * *

"'Pauline' did not take its place among the author's collected works until 1867, when the uniform edition of them appeared; and he then introduced it by a preface, in which he declared his unwillingness to publish such a boyish production, and gave the reasons which induced him to do so.   The poem is boyish, or at all events youthful, in point of conception; and we need not wonder that its intellectual crudeness should have outweighed its finished poetic beauties in the author's mind. It contains, however, one piece of mental portraiture, which, with slight modifications, might have stood for Mr. Browning when he re-edited the work as it clearly did when he wrote it.   It begins thus: 'I am made up of an intensest life.' The tribute to the saving power of imagination is also characteristic of his mature mind, though expressed in an ambiguous manner.   It is interesting to know that in the line 'The king treading the purple calmly to his death,' he was thinking of Agamemnon, as this shows how early his love of classic literature began.   The allusion to Plato largely confirms this impression.   The feeling for music asserts itself, though in a less spiritual form than it assumes in his later works.   The most striking piece of true biography which 'Pauline' contains, is its evidence of the young writer's reverent affection for Shelley, whom he idealizes under the name of Sun-treader.   An invocation to his memory occupies three pages, beginning with the eighth, and is renewed at the end of the poem. * * * The curious Latin quotation of the preface is from the works of Cornelius Agrippa, a well-known professor of occult philosophy, and is indeed introductory to a treatise upon it. * * * The Andromeda described as 'with the speaker,' is that of Caravaggio, of which Mr. Browning possesses an engraving which was always before his eyes as he wrote his earlier poems."—*Mrs. Orr.*

XLV.

The Red Cotton Nightcap Country.

"The real life drama, which Mr. Browning has reproduced under this title, was enacted partly in Paris and partly in a retired corner of Normandy, where he spent the late summer of 1872; and ended in a trial which had been only a fortnight closed, when he supposed himself to be relating it.   His whole story is true, except that in it which reality itself must have left to the imagination."—*Mrs. Orr.*

"It is the story of Mellario, the Paris jeweler, and was studied at the place of his ending, St. Aubin in Normandy, from the law papers used in the suit concerning his will. It was put in type with all the true names of persons and things; but, on a proof being submitted by Browning to his friend, Lord Coleridge, then attorney-general, the latter thought that an action for libel might lie for what was said in the poem, however unlikely it was that such procedure would be taken. Thereupon fictitious names were substituted."—*L. Br. S. Papers.*

The possible friend and adviser, to whom Miranda is referred, was M. Joseph Milsand, who always at that time passed the bathing season at St. Aubin.

XLVI.

Fifine at the Fair.

XLVII.

The Inn Album.

This poem is, in the main outlines, a true story, that of Lord de Ros, once a friend of the great Duke of Wellington and about whom there is much in the Gréville memoirs. The story made a great sensation in London over thirty years ago.

XLVIII.

Sordello.

XLIX.

The Ring and the Book.

Note.—Experience would indicate that the most effective way of studying the last two is to assign the lesson beforehand, which in the case of "The Ring and the Book" may reasonably cover a book; this to be carefully studied by each individual at home; then, when they come together, to compare notes, and each contribute his mite to the general whole in some such order as follows:—

1. Tell the story.
2. Its relation to the preceding lessons.
3. What new elements introduced into the story by this lesson.
4. What chief moral lesson found by each.
5. Noblest passages and quotable lines.
6. Difficult passages.
7. Out-of-the-way words and allusions.

After such a study as this, then and only then will the club be prepared either to write or to listen to some papers upon general topics, including a range of the whole work. Only where classes are comparatively small, of uniform grade of intelligence and socially familiar and congenial, is it wise to undertake to read in class.

SHORTER PROGRAMMES.

These short programmes are prepared for the use of those who have not the time or do not desire to make a complete study of Browning, but would like to gain some knowledge of his poems. It is impossible to prepare any partial list of these poems that is wholly representative of the poet and his best work, and it should be borne in mind that such lists are necessarily subject to the particular mental bias and preference of the individual preparing them, and are thus fit matter for the revision of any other student of Browning. For notes on the poems, see full classification.

With regard to the classification of Browning's poems, it should be said that all classifications are more or less arbitrary, and that most of the poems fall naturally into more than one group. The reader need not therefore be surprised at finding certain poems placed under different heads in the three programmes.

PROGRAMME A.

I.

Love Poems.

1. Wedded Love.

One Word More.
A Woman's Last Word.
Any Wife to Any Husband.

Two in the Campagna.
By the Fireside.
A Lover's Quarrel.

2. Love and Tragedy.

The Last Ride Together.
Youth and Art.
The Laboratory.

The Confessional.
In a Balcony.
James Lee's Wife.

3. Love Lyrics.

Meeting at Night.
Parting at Morning.
One Way of Love.
Another Way of Love.
Love Among the Ruins.
Natural Magic, Magical Nature.
Never the Time and the Place.

My Star.
Love in a Life.
Life in a Love.
In Three Days.
In a Year.
The Worst of it.
Too Late.

II.

Poems on Art.

Andrea del Sarto. √
Fra Lippo Lippi.
Old Pictures in Florence.
The Guardian Angel.
Pictor Ignotus.

III.

Poems on Music.

A Toccato of Galuppi's.
Master Hugues of Saxe-Gotha.
Abt Vogler.

IV.

Poems Illustrating Browning's Ideas of the Poetic Art.

How it Strikes a Contemporary.
House.
Shop.
Epilogue, " The Poets Give Us Wine."
At the Mermaid.

V.

Poems of Early Christian Art.

The Epistle.
Death in the Desert.

VI.

Poems of Immortality and Religious Life.

La Saisiaz.
Christmas Eve.
Easter Day.
Evelyn Hope.
May and Death.
Prospice.
Rabbi Ben Ezra.

VII.

Other Religious Poems.
Caliban on Setebos.
Saul.

VIII.

Heroes and Heroines.
The Patriot. ✓
Hervé Riel. ✓
Echetlos.
Incident of the French Camp. ✓
The Lost Leader.

IX.

Jewish Life and Character.
Holy Cross Day.
Jochanan Hakkadosh.
Burial Privilege of Baldinucci.

X.

Psychological.
[Only a few of the most striking short poems have been placed under this head, which is descriptive in a certain sense of all that Browning ever wrote.]
Ned Bratts.
Halbert and Hob.
Martin Relph.
Soliloquy of the Spanish Cloister.
Gold Hair.
A Light Woman. ✓
The Statue and the Bust.

PROGRAMME B.

This programme is made up of some of the long single poems and a few of the dramas, and necessarily includes two or three mentioned in the foregoing programmes.

   I.   Bishop Blougram's Apology.
   II.   Caliban on Setebos.
   III.   Saul.
   IV.   James Lee's Wife.
   V.   In a Balcony.
   VI.   Fifine at the Fair.
   VII.   A Blot in the 'Scutcheon.
   VIII.   Martin Relph.
   IX.   The Flight of the Duchess.
   X.   Ivan Ivanovitch.
   XI.   Luria.
   XII.   A Soul's Tragedy.
   XIII.   Pippa Passes.
   XIV.   Paracelsus.

CHRONOLOGICAL LIST

OF

ROBERT BROWNING'S WORKS.

Born 1812, at Camberwell, England.

1833.   Pauline.
1835.   Paracelsus.
1837.   Strafford.
1840.   Sordello.

1841. Pippa Passes. (Bells and Pomegranates, No. I.)
1842. King Victor and King Charles. (B. and P. No. II.)
1842. Dramatic Lyrics. (B. and P. No. III.)

Cavalier Tunes.
 Marching along.
 Give a Rouse.
 My Wife Gertrude.
Italy and France.
 Italy; or, My Last Duchess.
 France; or, Count Gismond.
Camp and Cloister.
 Camp (French.)
 Cloister (Spanish.)
In a Gondola.
Artemis Prologuizes.
Waring.
Queen Worship.
 Rudel and the Lady of Tripoli.
 Christina.
Mad-House Cell.
 Johannes Agricola.
 Porphyria.
Through the Metidja.
The Pied Piper of Hamelin.

1843. Return of the Druses. (B. and P. No. IV.)
1843. A Blot in the 'Scutcheon. (B. and P. No. V.)
1844. Colombe's Birthday. (B. and P. No. VI.)
1844–5. Seven Poems in " Hood's Magazine."

The Laboratory.
Claret.
Tokay.
Sibrandus Schnafnaburgensis.
The Boy and the Angel.
The Tomb at St. Praxed's.
The Flight of the Duchess.

1845.   Dramatic Romances and Lyrics. (B. and P. No. VII.

> How They Brought the Good News.
> Pictor Ignotus.
> Italy in England.
> England in Italy.
> The Lost Leader.
> The Lost Mistress.
> Home Thoughts from Abroad.
> The Confessional.
> Earth's Immortalities.
> Song, " Nay, but you."
> Night and Morning.
> Saul.
> Time's Revenges.
> The Glove.

1845.   Luria,
        A Soul's Tragedy, } (B. and P. No. VIII.)

1846.   Married to Elizabeth Barrett.

1849.   Revised his printed poems.

1850.   Christmas Eve and Easter Day.

1852.   Prose Essay on Shelley.

1855.   Men and Women.

Series 1.

Love Among the Ruins.	A Pretty Woman.
A Lover's Quarrel.	Childe Roland.
Evelyn Hope.	Respectability.
Up at a Villa—Down in the City.	A Light Woman.
A Woman's Last Word.	The Statue and the Bust.
Fra Lippo Lippi.	Love in a Life.
A Toccata of Galluppi's.	Life in a Love.
By the Fireside.	Instans Tyrannus.
Any Wife to Any Husband.	My Star.
An Epistle of Karshish.	The Last Ride Together.
A Serenade at the Villa.	The Patriot.
How it Strikes a Contemporary.	Memorabilia.
Master Hugues of Saxe Gotha.	Mesmerism.
Bishop Blougram's Apology.	

Series II.

Andrea del Sarto.	Before.
After.	In Three Days.
In a Year.	Old Pictures in Florence.
In a Balcony.	Saul.
De Gustibus.	Women and Roses.
Protus.	Holy-Cross Day.
The Guardian Angel.	Cleon.
The Twins.	Popularity.
The Heretic's Tragedy.	Two in the Campagna.
A Grammarian's Funeral.	One Way of Love.
Another Way of Love.	Transcendentalism.
Misconceptions.	One Word More.

1861. Death of Mrs. Browning.

1864. Dramatis Personæ.

James Lee.
Gold Hair.
The Worst of It.
Dis Aliter Visum.
Too Late.
Abt Vogler.
Rabbi Ben Ezra.
A Death in the Desert.
Caliban Upon Setebos.
Confessions.
Prospice.
Youth and Art.
A Face.
A Likeness.
Mr. Sludge.
Apparent Failure.
Epilogue.

1868-9. The Ring and the Book.

1871. Hervé Riel.

1871. Balaustion's Adventure.

1871. Prince Hohenstiel-Schwangau.

1872. Fifine at the Fair.
1873. Red Cotton Night-Cap Country.
1875. Aristophanes' Apology.
1875. The Inn Album.
1876. Pacchiarotto and Other Poems.

> Prologue.
> Pacchiarotto.
> At the Mermaid.
> House.
> Shop.
> Pisgah Sights, I and II.
> Fears and Scruples.
> Natural Magic.
> Magical Nature.
> Bifurcation.
> Numpholeptos.
> Appearances.
> St. Martin's Summer.
> A Forgiveness.
> Cenciaja.
> Filippo Baldinucci.
> Epilogue.

1877. Agamemnon.
1878. La Saisiaz.
        The Two Poets of Croisic.
1880. Dramatic Idyls.

Series I.

Martin Relph.	Pheidippides.
Halbert and Hob.	Ivan Ivanovitch.
Tray.	Ned Bratts.

Series II.

Proem.	Echetlos.
Clive.	Muleykeh.
Pietro of Abano.	Doctor ———.
Pan and Luna.	Epilogue.

1883. Jocoseria.

- Wanting is—What?
- Donald.
- Solomon and Balkis.
- Cristina and Monaldeschi.
- Mary Wolstonecroft and Fuseli.
- Adam, Lilith and Eve.
- Ixion.
- Jochanan Hakkadosh.
- Never the Time and the Place.
- Pambo.

1885. Ferishtah's Fancies.

HELPS TO THE STUDY OF BROWNING.

Richard Grant White's saying, that the way to read Shakespeare is to read him, is good advice and applicable to the one who would make a study of Robert Browning. Most of the critical studies published are found in magazines and reviews, a full list of which may be found in Poole's Index. Among the available books that may be of use are the following:

Browning Society Papers.   See page 41.

Handbook to the Works of Robert Browning, by Mrs. Sutherland Orr.

Stories from Robert Browning, by Frederic May Holland.

See also the essays on Browning in "Obiter Dicta," Stedman's "Victorian Poets," George W. Cooke's "Poets and Problems" and Professor Dowden's "Studies in Literature."

BROWNING SOCIETIES.

The so-called Browning movement was inaugurated by the organization of the London Browning Society in July, 1881, and includes men of the highest rank and scholarship among its members. Through its publications and other activities it has done much effective work in awakening an interest in these writings and encouraging organizations for their study. Jenkin Lloyd Jones, 3939 Langley avenue, Chicago, is the local Honorary Secretary of this society. In ———— Prof. Corson, of Cornell University, organized a Browning Society at Ithaca, N. Y. Prof. Levi Thaxter previous to this time had had various classes for the study of Robert Browning in and around Boston. In November, 1882, the first Browning club was organized in Chicago, which in four years' work has included in its study all his writings. From this club, more or less directly, seven or eight other circles have sprung up in the city and vicinity, and perhaps as many more in other cities throughout the west. On the fourteenth of April, 1886, the Chicago workers organized themselves into the Chicago Browning Society, for the purpose of mutual help and with the hope of encouraging wider study. The society will hold monthly meetings during winter months, and will from time to time publish such helps as its funds will warrant, this pamphlet being the first of the series. See programme for this season, page 50. It has arranged with Charles H. Kerr & Co., 175 Dearborn street, to become its publishers. This firm is also agent for the London Society, and is prepared to fill any orders for Browning material. Correspondence solicited.

RULES FOR LITERARY CLUBS.

The following "ten commandments" for the guidance of literary studies have been found helpful, and are here reprinted as a suggestion to new clubs.

I.

Aim to study, not to create, literature.

II.

Avoid red tape and parliamentary slang.

III.

Let but one talk at a time, and that one talk only of the matter in hand.

IV.

Start no side conferences: whispering is poor wisdom and bad manners.

V.

Come prepared. Let the work be laid out systematically in deliberate courses of reading and study.

VI.

Let papers be short. Beware of long quotations. "Brevity is the soul of wit."

VII.

Be as willing to expose ignorance as to parade knowledge.

VIII.

Aim not to exhaust, but to open the theme. Incite curiosity. Provoke home reading.

IX.

Begin and close to the minute.

X.

Meet all discouragements with grit and industry. Rise superior to numbers; for the kingdom of culture, like the kingdom of God, comes without observation.

BROWNING AND THE CRITICS.

If Browning has had his detractors he has also always had his admirers, men of genius and wide attainment like himself, who are quick to recognize in him one of the leading and most prolific minds of the age. Such intelligent and generous commendation amply atones for the loss of popular applause. Below is a short list of extracts from leading critics, selected for the most part from the trial list of criticisms published in the Browning Society Papers, parts I and II.

" To be a poet is to have a soul so quick to discern that no shade of quality escapes it, and so quick to feel that discernment is but a hand playing with finely ordered variety on the chord of emotion, a soul in which knowledge passes instantaneously into feeling, and feeling flashes back as a new organ of knowledge."—*George Eliot on Robert Browning.*

" It is some time since we read a work of more unequivocal power than ' Paracelsus.' We conclude that its author is a young man, as we do not recollect his having published before. If so, we may safely predict for him a brilliant career, * * * if he continues true to the promise of his genius. He possesses all the elements of a fine poet."
—*John Forster, in Examiner, Sept., 1835.*

" Without the slightest hesitation we name Robert Browning at once with Shelley, Coleridge and Wordsworth. * * * He has in himself all the elements of a great poet, philosophical as well as dramatic."—*Ibid, in Monthly Magazine, 1836.*

" By far the richest nature of our times."—*J. R. Lowell before the Browning Society.*

" I would rather have written the " Blot in the 'Scutcheon " than any other work of modern times. There is no other man living who could produce such a work."—*Charles Dickens.*

" Browning! Since Chaucer was alive and hale,
No man has walked along our road with step
So active, so inquiring eye, or tongue
So varied in discourse."

—From Sonnet by W. S. Landor.

" Everything Browningish is found here—the legal jauntiness, the knitted argumentation, the cunning prying into detail, the suppressed tenderness, the humanity, the salt intellectual humor. * * Whatever else may be said of Mr. Browning and his work by way of criticism, it will be admitted on all hands that *nowhere in literature can be found a man and a work more fascinating in their way.* As for the man, he was crowned long ago, and we are not one of those who grumble because one king has a better seat than another, an easier cushion, a finer light in the great temple. A king is a king and each will choose his place."
—Robert Buchanan on "The Ring and the Book," in Athenæum, Dec. 1868.

" Unerring in every sentence; always vital, right, profound. * * In a single poem, 'The Bishop Orders his Tomb,' Browning tells nearly all that I have said of the central Renaissance in thirty pages of 'Stones of Venice.' "*—Ruskin.*

"Now if there is any great quality more perceptible than another in Mr. Browning's intellect, it is his decisive and incisive quality of thought, his sureness and intensity of perception, his rapid and trenchant resolution of aim. To charge him with obscurity is about as correct as to call Lynceus purblind or to complain of the slowness of the telegraphic wires. He is something too much the reverse of obscure ; he is too brilliant and subtle for the ready reader of a ready writer to follow with any certainty the track of an intelligence which moves with such incessant rapidity."*—A. C. Swinburne, in introduction to works of George Chapman.*

"Of all writers since Dante we should speak of Browning as the poet of suffering, suffering on a great scale, though impelled and passion-wrought."*—Eclectic and Congregational Review, Dec., 1868.*

"To blend a profound knowledge of human nature, a keen perception of the awful problem of human destiny, with the conservation of a joyous human spirit, to know and not despair of them, to battle with one's spiritual foes and not be broken by them is given only to the very strong. This is to be a valiant and unvanquished soldier of humanity."*—Edinburgh Review, July, 1869.*

" He is chiefly dear to the age because having been racked with its doubts, stretched upon the mental torture wheels of its despair, having sounded cynicism and pessimism to their depths, he sometimes firmly and sometimes faintly trusts the larger hope, but always, in the last analysis and residuum of thought, trusts. Coming from such a mind, such a buoyant message this vexed and storm-tossed age will not willingly let die."—*H. R. Haweis.*

" He is the intellectual phenomenon of the last half century, even if he is not the poetical aloe of modern English literature. His like we have never seen before. * * * In all true poetry the form of the thought is part of the thought, and never was this absolute law of literary æsthetics more flagrantly illustrated than in the poetry of Robert Browning. To say that Browning is the greatest dramatic poet since Shakespeare is to say that he is the greatest poet, most excellent in what is the highest form of imaginative composition, because it is the most creative."—*Richard Grant White.*

" In considering whether a poet is intelligible and lucid we ought not to grope and grub about his work in search of obscurities and oddities, but should, in the first instance at all events, attempt to regard his whole scope and range, to form some estimate, if we can, of his general purport and effect, asking ourselves how are we the better for him, has he quickened any passion, lightened any burden, purified any taste, does he play any real part in our lives? And if we are compelled to answer "Yes" to such questions, it is both folly and ingratitude to complain of obscurity."—*Augustine Birrell in " Obiter Dicta."*

LECTURES AND PAPERS.

The following papers and lectures are probably available, with the necessary restrictions of time and place, to circles, classes or clubs or popular audiences interested in the study of Browning. Prof. Louis J. Block, of the Douglas school, Chicago, Rev. David Utter, 115 Twenty-third street, and Jenkin Lloyd Jones, 3939 Langley avenue, have lectures on the general subject of Browning and his writings. Mr. Utter also gives special interpretations and readings. Mr. Jones has special papers on "Fifine at the Fair," "Christmas Eve and Easter Day," "A Soul's Tragedy," "The Religion of Browning," and will give conversations, help organize clubs, etc.

Mrs. S. C. Ll Jones, No. 3939 Langley avenue, has papers on " Luria" and " The Tragedies of Love."

Mrs E T. Leonard, No. 175 Dearborn street, has papers on "Mildred Tresham," "Djabal" and "Browning's Measure of Life and his Standard of Success."

Mrs. Emma E. Marean, No. 3619 Ellis avenue, has papers on "The Poet-pair," "A Study of Clara" (in the "Red Cotton Night-Cap Country,") Ferishtah's Fancies," and " Browning's Interpretation of the Poet's Mission."

Miss Mary E. Burt, 3410 Rhodes avenue, has a paper on "Sordello."

Mrs Anna B McMahan, of Quincy, Ill., gives lectures and interpretations of the writings of Robert Browning.

James Colgrove, 134 Wabash avenue, has made a special study of ' Old Pictures in Florence," and has a collection of illustrative pictures.

(46)

THE CHICAGO BROWNING SOCIETY.

The first club for the study of Robert Browning's writings was organized in Chicago in the autumn of 1882. This club has continued its systematic course of study of these writings for the last four years, and from this more or less directly have sprung seven or eight other circles in this city and immediate vicinity, and perhaps as many more in a like manner throughout the west. Believing that the time had come when these unrelated workers might profitably accomplish something in a co-operative way, a call was issued, signed by fifty ladies and gentlemen, most of them members of these Chicago Browning Circles, for a meeting to be held in the parlors of the Church of the Messiah, April 14, 1886. Over a hundred persons were present. A paper was read on the writings of Robert Browning by Prof. L. J. Block; readings were given by Mrs. F. W. Parker and David Utter, followed by a song from G. E. Dawson, Esq; after which the organization was perfected as below.

The officers were instructed to arrange for the beginning of the active work of the society in the autumn of 1886.

CONSTITUTION.

ARTICLE I. The name of this Association shall be the Chicago Browning Society.

ARTICLE II. The object of this Society shall be to promote the reading and study of Robert Browning's works, the publication of helps in such study, and other matters calculated to awaken a wider interest in this poet.

ARTICLE III. Any person interested may become an annual member by the payment of two dollars and fifty cents ($2.50), the payment of which shall give each member the right to attend all regular meetings of the society, and to a copy of all the publications issued during the year. Any one may become a life member of this society by the payment at one time of twenty-five dollars ($25.00).

ARTICLE IV. The officers of this society shall be a president, three vice-presidents, a secretary, a treasurer, and nine other persons, forming an executive committee, three of which shall constitute a sub-committee on publication. These officers shall be elected annually, their duties shall be such as usually devolve upon such officers in similar societies; they shall hold office until their successors are chosen, and the executive committee shall have power to fill vacancies in the committee, to call meetings, etc., and to them shall be entrusted the general management of the affairs of the society, provided a majority shall be necessary to form a quorum for the transaction of business.

ARTICLE V. The Society shall hold at least four meetings in each year, the annual meeting being on the second Tuesday in April, at which time the annual dues must be paid.

ARTICLE VI. This Constitution may be amended by a majority vote at any regular meeting, providing two months notice of the same be sent to each member through post-office, or otherwise.

OFFICERS FOR 1886-7.

President—Jenkin Lloyd Jones.

Vice-Presidents—Mrs. Wirt Dexter, Mrs. Wm. L. McCormick, Mrs. Celia P. Woolley.

Secretary—Mrs. Ellen Mitchell, 44 Sixteenth Street.

Treasurer—Mrs. Reginald de Koven, 99 Pearson Street.

Directors.

David Utter,	Louis J. Block,	James Colegrove,
Miss Grace T. Howe,	Mrs. Potter Palmer,	Mrs. Emma E. Marean,
Mrs. H. A. Johnson,	Mrs. A. N. Eddy,	Mrs. F. S. Parker.

Committee on Publication.

Rev. David Utter,	Mrs. Emma E. Marean,	Mrs. C. P. Woolley.

CHARTER MEMBERS.

Mrs. Mary N. Adams,
Miss Mary E. Burt,
Mrs. Amanda N. Beiss,
Mrs. H. J. Beckwith,
Mrs. J. C. Brooks,
Prof. L. J. Block,
Miss E. W. Brown,
James Colegrove,
Mrs. A. J. Caton,
Mrs. John M. Clark,
Miss L. M. Dunning,
Mrs. Wirt Dexter,
Mrs. Ruth B. Ewing,
Mrs. A. N. Eddy,
C. Norman Fay,
Chas. A. Gregory,
Mrs. Chas. A. Gregory,
Robert J. Hendricks,
Franklin H. Head,
Mrs. John J. Herrick,
Chas. D. Hamill,
Mrs. Susan W. Hamill,
Mrs. Ellen Henrotin,
Miss Grace Howe,
Miss May Henderson,
Jenkin Lloyd Jones,
Mrs. S. C. Lloyd Jones,
Mrs. Frank Johnson,
Mr. Hosmer A. Johnson,
Mr. John H. Jewett,
Mrs. John H. Jewett,
Charles H. Kerr,
Mrs. E. W. Kohlsaat

Reginald de Koven,
Mrs. R. de Koven,
Miss Susie King,
William S. Lord,
Miss Martha J. Loudon,
Miss Mary L. Lord,
Miss Julia Leavens,
C. P. Morgan,
Mrs. Emma E. Marean,
Mrs. Anna Morgan,
Mrs. W. T. McCormick,
Mrs. R. Hall McCormick,
Mrs. Ellen Mitchell,
Mrs. Franklin MacVeagh,
Mr. Franklin MacVeagh,
Mr. A. R. Parker,
Mrs. F. S. Parker,
Mr. F. W. Parker,
Mrs. Alice H. Putnam,
Mrs. Potter Palmer,
Potter Palmer,
Mrs. R. W. Patterson, Jr.,
Mrs. D. F. Sellbridge,
B. D. Slocum,
Miss Helen D. Street,
Miss Carrie Smith,
Mrs A. T. Spalding,
Mrs. A. N. Stevenson,
Laura J. Tisdale,
Rev. David Utter,
Miss Jennie A. Willcox,
Mrs. Celia P. Woolley,
Mrs J. M. Walker.

PLAN OF WORK FOR 1886-7.

The meetings of this Society will be held the second Tuesday of each month at eight o'clock P. M., beginning in November and ending in May. Three of these will be public meetings, four for study and for members only. The following is the programme for the coming season.

NOVEMBER (PUBLIC).

Introductory Meeting—paper by Rev. Jenkin Lloyd Jones.

DECEMBER.

Subject to be announced.

JANUARY (PUBLIC).

Reading of one of Browning's plays by members of the Society.

FEBRUARY.

Browning's Interpretation of Old Age—paper by Prof. David Swing.

MARCH (PUBLIC).

Dramatic Performance by members of the Society.

APRIL.

Annual Meeting.

MAY.

Four papers on Ivan Ivanovitch—writers, Mrs. Dexter, Mrs. Mitchell, Mr. Head, Mr. Gilbert.

Due notice of the place of meeting will be given.

Applications for membership should be made to the Treasurer.

www.ingramcontent.com/pod-product-compliance
Lightning Source LLC
Chambersburg PA
CBHW030903260626
47169CB00008B/2656